Walt Disney's Cinderella

Illustrated by Ron Dias and Bill Lorencz

 A GOLDEN BOOK • NEW YORK

Copyright © 1998, 2005 Disney Enterprises, Inc. All rights reserved under International and Pan-American Copyright Conventions. Published in the United States by Golden Books, an imprint of Random House Children's Books, a division of Random House, Inc., New York, and simultaneously in Canada by Random House of Canada Limited, Toronto, in conjunction with Disney Enterprises, Inc. Originally published in different form by Golden Books Publishing Company in 1998. Golden Books, A Golden Book, A Little Golden Book, the G colophon, and the distinctive gold spine are registered trademarks of Random House, Inc.

Library of Congress Control Number: 2005921522

ISBN: 0-7364-2362-1

www.goldenbooks.com   www.randomhouse.com/kids/disney

Printed in the United States of America   10 9 8 7

Once upon a time, in a faraway kingdom, there lived a widowed gentleman and his lovely daughter, Ella.

Ella was a beautiful girl. She had golden hair, and her eyes were as blue as forget-me-nots.

The gentleman was a kind and devoted father, and he
gave Ella everything her heart desired. But he felt she
needed a mother. So he married again, choosing for his wife
a woman who had two daughters. Their names were
Anastasia and Drizella.

The gentleman soon died. Then the Stepmother's true nature was revealed. She was only interested in her mean, selfish daughters.

The Stepmother gave Ella a little room in the attic, old rags to wear, and all the housework to do. Soon everyone called her Cinderella, because when she cleaned the fireplaces, she was covered with cinders.

But Cinderella had many friends. The old horse and Bruno the dog loved her. The mice loved her, too. She protected them from her Stepmother's nasty cat, Lucifer. Two of her favorite mice were Gus and Jaq.

Cinderella was kind to everyone—even to Lucifer. But Lucifer took advantage of her kindness.

Lucifer liked to get Cinderella in trouble. One morning, he chased Gus onto Anastasia's breakfast tray. She screamed and blamed Cinderella.

"Come here," the Stepmother said to Cinderella. "The windows—wash them! Then scrub the terrace, sweep the halls, and, of course, there's the laundry."

In another part of the kingdom, the King was
worrying about his son. "It's high time he married and
settled down!" he told the Grand Duke.

"But sire," said the Grand Duke, "we must be patient."

"No buts about it!" shouted the King. "We'll have a
ball tonight. It will be very romantic. Send out the
invitations!"

When the invitation arrived, Cinderella's Stepmother announced, "There's a ball! In honor of the Prince . . . every eligible maiden is to attend."

"That means I can go, too!" Cinderella said.

"Well, I see no reason why you can't," the Stepmother replied with a sly smile. "If you get your work done, and if you can find something suitable to wear."

Cinderella had hoped to fix her old party dress, but Anastasia and Drizella wanted her to help them instead.

The Stepmother kept her busy, too.

Cinderella worked hard all day long. When she finally returned to her little attic room, it was almost time to leave for the ball. And her dress wasn't ready!

But the loyal mice had managed to find ribbons, sashes, ruffles, and bows. The mice had sewn them to her party dress, and it looked beautiful.

The stepsisters shrieked when they saw Cinderella. "They're my ribbons!" "That's my sash!" They tore her dress to shreds.

"Come along now, girls," said the Stepmother. And they left Cinderella behind.

Cinderella ran into the garden. She wept and wept.
Suddenly, a hush fell over the garden, and a cloud of
lights began to twinkle and glow around Cinderella's head.
"Come now, dry those tears," said a gentle voice. Then a
small woman appeared in the cloud. "You can't go to the
ball looking like that. What in the world did I do with that
magic wand?"

"Magic wand?" gasped Cinderella. "Then you must be . . ."

"Your Fairy Godmother," the woman replied, pulling her magic wand out of thin air. "The first thing you need is a . . . pumpkin."

A cloud of sparkles floated across the garden. A pumpkin rose up and swelled into an elegant coach. The mice turned into horses, the old horse became a coachman, and Bruno became a footman.

"Well, hop in, my dear," said the woman.

"But my dress . . . ," said Cinderella.

The Fairy Godmother looked at it. "Good heavens!" With a wave of her wand, she turned the rags into an exquisite gown. On Cinderella's feet were tiny glass slippers.

"You'll have only till midnight," the Fairy Godmother said. "At the stroke of twelve, the spell will be broken, and everything will be as it was before."

Cinderella promised to leave the ball on time. Then, under a shower of magic sparkles, she stepped into her coach and was swept away to the palace.

When Cinderella arrived at the ball, the Prince was
yawning with boredom. Then he caught sight of her.
    Ignoring everyone else, the Prince walked over to
Cinderella. He kissed her hand and asked her to dance.
They swirled off across the ballroom.

The Prince didn't leave Cinderella's side all night. They danced every dance together. As the lights dimmed and sweet music floated out into the summer night, Cinderella heard the clock begin to chime.

"Oh, goodness!" she gasped. "It's midnight. I must . . . Goodbye!"

"Wait! Come back!" called the Prince. "I don't even know your name!"

Cinderella hurried down the palace steps. In her haste, she lost one of the glass slippers, but she had no time to pick it up. She leaped into the waiting coach.

As soon as the coach went through the gates, the magic spell was broken. Cinderella found herself standing by the side of the road, dressed in her old rags. On one foot, she still wore a glass slipper.

Her coachman was an old horse again, and her footman was Bruno the dog. Her coach was a hollow pumpkin, and her horses were four of her mouse friends. They looked sadly at Cinderella.

They all hurried home. They had to be back before the others returned from the ball.

The next day, the Stepmother told the girls that the Grand Duke was coming to see them. "He's been hunting all night for that girl—the one who lost her slipper. That girl shall be the Prince's bride."

Cinderella smiled and hummed a waltz that had been played at the ball. The Stepmother became suspicious. She locked Cinderella in her room.

Gus and Jaq had a plan to help Cinderella. While Anastasia and Drizella tried to squeeze their big feet into the little glass slipper, the two mice sneaked into the Stepmother's pocket. They got hold of the key, tugged it upstairs, and unlocked the door. Cinderella rushed downstairs to try on the glass slipper.

"May I try it on?" Cinderella asked.

The wicked Stepmother fumed. She tripped the footman who was holding the glass slipper. It fell to the floor and broke into a thousand pieces.

"But you see," Cinderella said, reaching into her pocket, "I have the other slipper."

She put it on, and it fit perfectly!

From that moment on, everything was a dream come true. Cinderella went off to the palace with the happy Grand Duke. The Prince was overjoyed to see her, and so was the King.

Cinderella and the Prince were soon married.

In her happiness, Cinderella didn't forget about her animal friends. They all moved into the castle with her.

Everyone in the kingdom was delighted with the Prince's new bride. And Cinderella and the Prince lived happily ever after!